Stories from the Woods and Wild Places

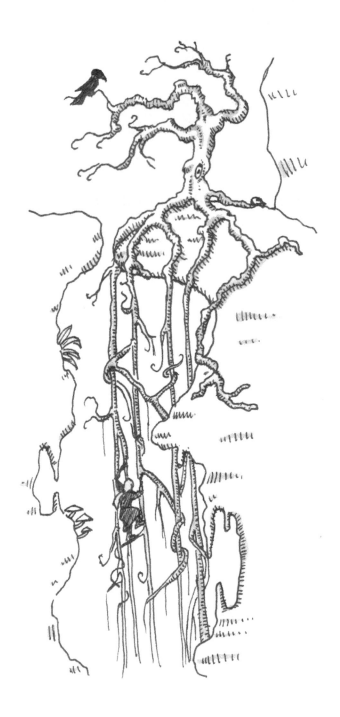

Stories from the Woods and Wild Places

Written and illustrated by Jason Buck

Jason Buck
2016

Copyright © 2016 by Jason Buck

All rights reserved. This book or any portion thereof may not be reproduced or used in any manner whatsoever without the express written permission of the publisher except for the use of brief quotations in a book review or scholarly journal.

Second Edition: 2016

First Printing: 2016

ISBN 978-1-326-56019-5

Jason Buck
9 Westbourne Mansions
Westbourne Crescent
Southampton, Hampshire SO17 1UW

www.JasonBuckStoryTeller.co.uk

Dedication

For my son Oskar

May you continue to create great adventures and, in turn, become a great adventurer yourself.

Contents

Acknowledgements ix
Foreword xi
The Loom 1
Anastasia 19
The Lost Lady of The Pines 33
The Toad's Tale 41
The Kelpie's Bridle 53

Acknowledgements

Thank you to my parents, for filling my childhood with stories and plays and puppets.

Thank you to my friend Teresa for opening the doors to storytelling in the mid 1990s.

Thank you to Louise for setting the stories free.

Thank you to my new friend Mike Rogers, academic, raconteur and storyteller extraordinaire, for enthusiasm, encouragement and opportunity.

Foreword

This is a collection of original fairy tales. You will recognise influences from traditional fairy tales and folklore from the UK, Russia and Western Europe, but the tales themselves are served fresh from the story mill.

These stories were originally created to be told aloud, performed to an audience, and I would encourage anyone to continue this ancient tradition of entertainment and communication, for all that it brings to both teller and listener.

Whether you read from a book, or speak from memory, remember it is not the individual words that are important, but putting yourself (and your listeners should you have them) into the experience of the story itself.

Enjoy these stories and then share them with others.

Jason

The Loom

There once was a widow. Sadly, her husband had died not long into their marriage, killed in battle in a far off place, for a far off nobleman, and all she had to remember him by was a scroll and small medal. She was, however, still young and beautiful; but beauty was not her greatest gift.

She was a weaver. The most wonderful weaver her country had ever seen, or was ever likely to see.

They say that as she moved the shuttle through the strings of the loom's warp, back and forth, back and forth, her fingers made music, as if she were playing a harp. They say that the threads of the weft that made up the cloth were magical and that the intricate designs and patterns she would weave could dance, could hold the summer sun and make it shine warm from the cloth in the depths of winter, could lull a baby to sleep, charm a lover to greater ardor or, if hung as curtains over a window or a door, they would hang like a shutter of steel against the night and all its horrors.

But this was not her greatest gift.

The young widow considered her greatest gift to be her children: A boy and a girl; twins. The boy, Pyotr, was strong and brave. The girl, Petra, was quick witted and courageous. And it was these two children the widow valued above all else in the world.

The little family lived well, with the widow's weaving providing money and respect in abundance, but the woman longed for the love of a man, to share her bed and to be a Father for her children, and in time she met a travelling man – a merchant.

His hair was as golden as the coins the widow gave to him, and his tongue as silver as the buckles and buttons she bought him. He could charm the birds from the trees and the sparkle in his eyes dazzled the widow and she fell helplessly in love.

But, as you may have already guessed, their marriage was not a happy one. As soon as his boots were under the table his silver tongue turned sharp and the sparkle in his eyes often turned to dazzle other young women in the village. He would spend the weaver woman's coin in the local tavern and return home late, snarling like a dog and bruising her fine features with his drunkard's fists.

Night after night, week after week, month after month the merchant's behaviour became worse and worse, his rages stronger and stronger.

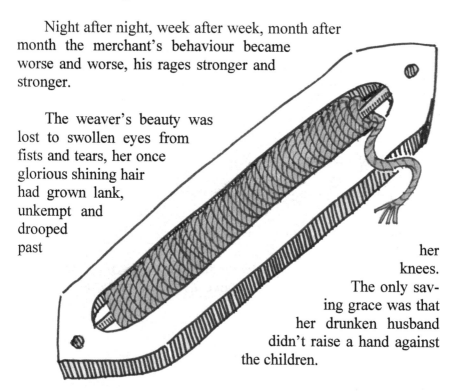

The weaver's beauty was lost to swollen eyes from fists and tears, her once glorious shining hair had grown lank, unkempt and drooped past her knees. The only saving grace was that her drunken husband didn't raise a hand against the children.

Until one night.

Coming home drunk and demanding his supper, the boy, Pyotr, looked away in disgust at his Stepfather's condition. Of course, this angered the man and in his spite he lashed out at the boy, knocking him to the floor!

His sister rushed between them, standing small but defiant, protecting her brother. As their Stepfather raised his hand to strike Petra, there was a sickening metallic thud as their Mother struck *him*, full on the head, with a heavy skillet, full of hot goose fat.

Their Mother, enraged, defending her children, raised the skillet a second time, but without waiting to see what would happen and not wanting to be struck again by the drunkard, the children threw open the door and fled out into the snow.

* * *

The night sky was cloud-blanketed and black, with slow-

falling pearls of heavy, white snowflakes. The light of a full moon, hiding her face behind the clouds gave the forest a ghostly-grey cast, the pale bones of trees thrusting up from the icy ground. The twins trudged on through deep snow, neither saying out loud what both knew in their hearts: they had left the path long ago and were lost.

A distant howl made both look up, eyes wide with fear, but then they noticed a friendly light in the distance, through the trees – a candle or torch, maybe a hearth fire – and they struggled on towards it.

Fingers stiff and toes burning with cold, Pyotr and his sister Petra got closer and closer to the light, until they could see it was the warm glow of a fire from a cottage window.

What they couldn't see was that the heavy snow hid the crookedness of the cottage's roof and walls, and lay so thick in the dark night so as to cover a fence of bones and conceal gateposts topped with small human skulls.

Shivering and shaking in the freezing night, they reached the cottage door and knocked as confidently as they could. If it were possible, the silence seemed to deepen. Moments passed and the only noise was the chattering of the children's teeth, then the door creaked open the merest crack, pushing snow ahead of it and allowing a spike of golden light to fall across their eyes, and the smell of wood smoke wafting temptingly into their nostrils, reminding them of happier days at home with their Mother.

"Who is it?" said a voice that sounded as old and gnarled as ancient tree branches rubbing in an autumn wind.

"My name is Pyotr and this is my sister Petra", said the boy in a voice that was not nearly as brave as he'd hoped.

"On your own?" cracked the voice. "At night? In the forest? And so far away from the path?"

"Yes", said Petra, gripping Pyotr's hand to share courage for the both of them. "We're very cold and hungry. May we come inside?".

"Hungry? Hmmm ... ", came the thoughtful reply.

A hesitation, and then the door opened with the cottage's occupant hidden behind it. Inside, the twins saw a great iron range, a fire blazing in its belly and a mighty pot of stew boiling and bubbling on top.

They barely heard the whispered ushering, "Come in … Come in …", but staggered into the little one-roomed building, heading straight for the range, their hands outstretched, reaching for the warmth.

They definitely didn't hear the quiet chuckle of the cottager, or the door bar sliding into place. The children fell to their knees, relishing the tingle as life and warmth returned to their smiling cheeks and aching hands.

But their joy at being rescued from the cruel, winter-dark forest was short-lived, as Pyotr was yanked from the floor by his collar.

Petra spun round to see a *very* tall woman, dressed in ragged cloaks and patched dresses.

All that was visible of her was her scrawny hands with lumpen knuckles and finger joints like stones under her skin, and a long hooked nose that protruded from the depths of her hood. She was incredibly strong, holding the kicking, thrashing Pyotr in mid air. Her head tipped back, cackling and revealing deep, dark-socketed eyes of further darkness, a chin that curved up almost to meet her nose and a puckered mouth surrounding sharp, cracked teeth.

Towering high above Petra, the hag held Pyotr up to her face and peered at him so closely he could smell her carrion breath, like an open grave. She licked her lips and tossed the boy into a cage in the corner of the room, as if he'd been a doll. She brushed Petra aside as the girl tried to help her brother, knocking her painfully into the wall, and strode over to slide home the cage door's bolt.

Pyotr strained against the bars of the cage, but the only effect was to make the hag laugh even louder. Once she had recovered herself, the great witch, for that was what she was, strode over to where Petra lay, crumpled and cowering. She leaned in so close that her curving sickle-beaked nose pressed against Petra's.

"Your brother will stay in that cage", she barked, "and you will cook and clean for me until … ". She paused and flicked a furtive look at Pyotr in the cage. "Well, until it's your turn for other things", she grinned nastily.

* * *

And so, with Pyotr caged, Petra did what the hag demanded out of fear for her brother's safety. But over the next few weeks something miraculous began to happen.

While the witch gave Pyotr more food than he could comfortably eat, poking and prodding him daily with her haggard claws and beating his sister when he tried to refuse more food, the strange and wicked woman cut off Petra's beautiful, golden hair.

But this wasn't the miracle.

Nor was it setting Petra to work at a great, crooked and twisted loom of brass that hummed with magic, where she demonstrated her Mother's great skill in weaving. Back and forth, back and forth went the shuttle, carrying the carded and twined strands of her own hair, making a cloth of the softest golden threads.

No. The miracle came the nights when Petra ran away.

After she had made Petra weave her own hair into cloth, and after she had forced Pyotr to eat to the point of bursting, and after she, herself, had eaten and left the scraps for Petra, the witch would lie down on a pallet of straw and furs and begin to snore like a woodsman sawing down a great oak.

Waiting until the snores started, Petra would creep to the door and, after showing her brother an expression of sympathy and solidarity, she would creep out into the night and run towards where she hoped her home village was, to get help.

The miracle happened every night that Petra escaped: Just as the light from the cottage window disappeared among the trees behind her, the witch would appear and catch her, grabbing her by her short-cropped hair. And as the witch grabbed and pulled at the ragged tufts, her hair stretched and grew until the witch was winding thick skeins of golden yellow over her arms, before dragging the girl back to the cottage and cutting off the silken lengths.

This went on for some time, with poor Petra becoming skinnier and poor Pyotr becoming fatter, until one night Petra found herself surprisingly awake. It was surprising as she had spent most of the previous night praying for help, and normally she was exhausted after completing the seemingly endless and arduous tasks the witch set her to.

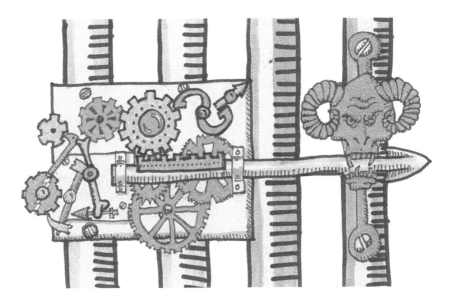

This night, while Petra lay awake, the witch quietly rose from her pallet, and walking with less noise than a cat's footfall, glided over to the cage in which Pyotr was sleeping. The girl watched through half-closed eyes, as the hag opened the complicated lock with very particular movements of her fingers and, without a noise, swung the cage door open, leaning in to sniff over the boy. She gently prodded him and, feeling how fat he had become, seemed satisfied.

"One more day. One more day will do", she hissed.

This made up Petra's mind. They both needed to escape the following night, before their fates were sealed.

* * *

The next day seemed to drag on forever.

Dutifully, and to keep her mind occupied, Petra swept and mopped, and scrubbed and washed, and dug and planted, and cooked and stitched, and chopped and stacked and, of course, wove.

Without being able to say much, she had managed to quickly whisper, "Tonight! Both of us! Our lives depend on it!" as she'd been sweeping near Pyotr's cage and the boy had had to suppress his excitement all day, despite his inactivity, so as not to give the witch any clue as to their plan.

As darkness fell, the fire in the range was banked to smolder through the night, and the cottage door was barred. Pyotr lay down and, after giving his sister a signal that he was ready, pretended to fall asleep. Petra curled in her corner, closing her eyes too and listening to the sounds in the room.

Finally ... finally ... the children heard the witch's breathing soften, deepen and rasp as she began to snore.

Heart thumping in her chest, Petra uncurled and padded across the floor and, with the same deft movements she'd seen the witch perform the night before, silently opened the lock on Pyotr's cage, and the boy crawled out.

Quiet as mice, they stole to the door and, as Petra softly lifted the wooden bar as she'd become practiced in her many previous escape attempts, Pyotr picked up the hatchet that was used to cut firewood, grimly nodded to his sister, and they both stepped into the snowy night.

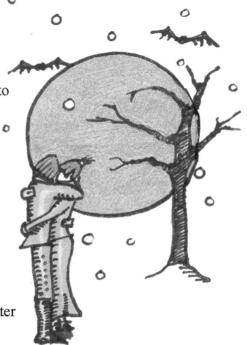

Flakes fell thick and fast – these would hide them – and the moon smiled down between rips in the clouds, a silvered lantern to show them the way home.

And they ran.

They ran as they'd never run before.

They ran, in the knowledge of what was behind them, maybe already pursuing them through the winter night.

Only a few minutes passed before they slowed, their young bodies tired – one fat and unfit from inactivity, the other thin and worn from over exertion.

They stopped.

And in the silence of the snow they held each other and felt the thrill of life and hope, sobbing into each other's shoulder.

Moments passed in the silent forest with only the sound of their slowing breathing and their tears of joy, pattering onto the snow, crusting in the freezing night.

And then She was there.

Where had she come from? There had been no sound of her approach, no trail of footsteps leading to where she now stood, but here was the great witch, terrible and exultant in her discovery of the escaped twins, towering, leering, sneering down at them.

"Run!" shouted Pyotr.

And they ran.

The children ran, blindly, spraying snow as they ran and stumbled, like a porpoise cutting through cresting waves.

The children ran and ran, but at the point of thinking they must have escaped, there she was again, but this time, the crone reached out and grabbed Petra's short-hacked hair. With a vicious yank not only did Petra's hair spill long and shining like a golden waterfall, but the girl was dragged to her knees.

She screamed, rising and running on, her hair continuing to flow behind her but, again, she was pulled to the floor, the witch cackling and screaming with wicked pleasure at the girl's struggles.

But the witch was enjoying herself a little too much.

She was so rapt, toying with Petra, that she didn't notice the girl's twin come up behind her. With a roar of fury beyond his years, Pyotr brought the hearth hatchet down with all his might, taking the hag's hand off at the wrist. The witch gave a terrifying, screaming shout of pain and anger. Wordless it echoed through the dark forest, shaking snow from the branches, raising owls from their perches, causing the animals who lived in holes and burrows to draw their young and loved ones closer and even making the trees weep sap as the sound cut into all things healthy and good.

The children had no time to wait. They were up and off in an instant, plunging ahead.

But evil is not always so easily killed and the witch's severed hand, still tangled in Petra's hair that flowed out far behind her, bumped and bounced along until it grabbed a tree root ... and held firm.

With the witch ploughing through the deep drifts with her long strides, red blood spraying from the wounded stump, Pyotr helped his sister up and both ran on, Petra's hair still cascading out behind her, like a fountain forced from a rock.

But this time, the children did *not* run blindly, or without help.

"This way!" said the Moon.

"That way!" hooted an Owl.

"Back!" creaked a Tree.

"And forth!" whispered the clouds.

"Back!" howled a distant wolf

"And forth!" called the Wind.

And so the two children ran, back and forth, back and forth, between the trees and the briars and the bushes, like a shuttle between the warp strings of a loom.

Back and forth, back and forth they ran, with Petra's hair threading through the forest, like weft on a loom, weaving a strong and powerful cloth.

Too late, the witch realised she was trapped, that she was bounded by Petra's hair, woven between the trees, making both a maze and a cage of her own. Her rage was terrible, but no matter how she railed against the woven threads, they gave and stretched, but they would not break and her fury could be heard for miles around.

Back and forth, back and forth the children continued to run until suddenly Petra was yanked from her feet and sat down hard on the snow. Her hair had stopped growing and she was now held fast.

Again, with a swiftness and strength that would make him a great warrior in later years, Pyotr brought down the axe, cutting clean through his sister's hair, freeing her.

But as he freed her, Petra's hair lost its golden sheen.

The hair on her head and the hair that wound through the briars and bushes and trees of the forest had turned white: White as snow, white as goose feathers, white as moonbeams.

And again they ran, this time hearing the witch's screams and rants growing quieter and quieter, losing her to the forest and her cage of silvered hair.

When they thought they could run no more, they saw the familiar lights of their home in the distance and there was their Mother, having heard the strange cries from the forest, standing in the light spilling from the door.

Seeing them she wept and rushed to hold them close. She took them inside and barred the door and the three held each other for many hours that night, until the warm sun rose, driving back the shadows to their corners, and brought with it the melting of icicles and the heads of snowdrops pushing up through the snow and the early signs of spring.

But what of the drunkard Stepfather? And what became of the witch?

Well, the Stepfather had mysteriously disappeared the night the children had fled into the forest. He was never seen again, but the twin's Mother treated herself to a new skillet.

No one knows what became of the witch, but if you walk through the forest at night and come across briars and bushes and trees, covered with a silvery-white down, with blood-red holly berries nearby, don't stop walking. Maybe the witch is still there, in the dark, dark forest, still trapped by Petra's silvered strands and howling her pain where Pyotr took her hand.

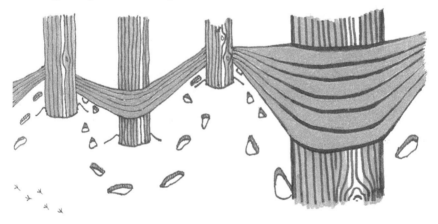

But for now, all you need to know is that while Pyotr grew to be a fine, strong and just soldier, even if he was always a little on the heavy side, Petra became a weaver of unparalleled skill.

It is said that she created tapestries that held and whispered the stories of her people, that she could make cloth that could keep out any cold, cloaks that could turn a spear point or catch an arrow and blankets that would hold a baby, calm, as if in its Mother's arms.

They both lived long and rich lives, and from that day on they always stayed on the path.

Anastasia

nastasia was only five when she got lost in the winter forest.

She had gone out with her parents on a sunny, crisp day when they had decided to brave the snow and see if they could find extra firewood in case they got snowed in, later in the season.

She was a good little girl with black hair and bright blue eyes and a loving nature, but she was still just a little girl and there were many other things in the snowy forest that were much more interesting than picking up heavy, icy sticks, which she left to her Mother and Father, while she explored.

There were logs to peer under or climb over, a croaking raven to chase and whirling eddies of snow to follow and each time she strayed away from her parents – and strayed from the path – they would call her back and admonish her for going so far away from them.

Of course, the first time she was told to stay in sight, and stay on the path, she instantly adhered to the parental command, until, of course, something interesting and distracting came along and then her attention would be solely focused on whatever that was.

Just as it started to snow great, soft, silent flakes, it was one particularly interesting leaf that tumbled along in an curling breeze, bouncing over the tree roots and crisp-crusted snow that shined so brightly in the winter sun, that took her just off the path and just out of site and then Anastasia was lost. For as soon as she was out of sight of her Mother and Father it didn't matter whether she was ten steps or ten miles away. Too young and inexperienced to follow her own footsteps back and too afraid of being scolded to cry out, she panicked and started running in the direction she thought her parents were, which, of course, was the wrong direction entirely.

To begin with, her Mother and Father thought she was playing a game or being cheeky, and called out for her to come back, but when she didn't return and the snow was starting to fall more heavily, they began to get worried and retraced their own steps to where little Anastasia had left the path.

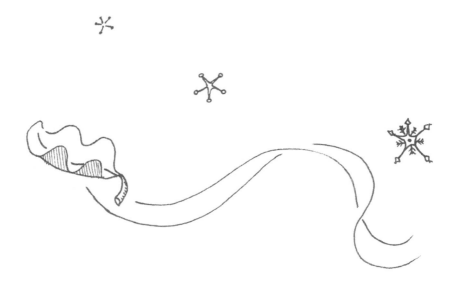

They could see the prints of her winter boots clearly to begin with, but quickly it became difficult to follow her, as she'd looped back, crossed over and created swirling patterns with her feet as she'd followed the tumbling leaf and the snow was filling in her little tracks.

Her Mother and Father now became really scared, calling out her name over and over again, but away from them, Anastasia heard their voices bouncing backwards and forwards between the trunks of the great trees and no matter which way she headed their voices only grew quieter and quieter until there was silence; that silence that only comes with deep snow, where nothing else makes a noise and all one can hear is the squeak and crunch of the snow underfoot and the sound of our own breathing.

Feeling very afraid and very alone, and for want of anything else to do, Anastasia just kept on walking, her heart thumping in her chest like a tiny bird trying to escape its cage.

She walked until she came upon a part of the forest she recognised. It was a cliff where, in the summer, a waterfall poured and splashed and pounded into a deep pool that fed off into a stream. Now, though, the stream and pool were covered with snow and had become part of the smooth, white, gently undulating forest floor. The waterfall itself was still visible, but frozen – a great, tall wall of ice with crags and spikes and icicles – water, caught in time, shining with a quality that sparkled and twinkled in the sunshine.

Anastasia knew this place from visits with her Grandfather, who'd been a respected shaman, before his death in the autumn, and who used to bring her here since she'd been a baby and allow her to skip and play in the summer forest, paddling in the pool or throwing stones into the water, while he dreamed and let his spirit journey to other worlds and converse with beings that most mortals only knew from fairy tales. She had always enjoyed her visits, particularly exploring the small cave that was behind the then rushing sheet of water, and it was here that she headed now, squeezing her small frame through the tiny gap between the wall of waterfall-ice and the cliff.

Inside the cave, out of the wind, she sat down with her back to the wall and, facing the translucent screen of blue-white ice, started to cry. As she cried, the biting winter air froze the tears into diamonds on her soft cheeks.

When you are five years old and lost and alone, you are very, very alone. Anastasia was now very, very alone.

* * *

Whether it was the girl's soulful, infant sobs, her Grandfather's spirit nearby or the forest itself taking pity on the lost child, something old and elemental was disturbed in its ancient sleep.

It shifted, its long and immeasurable, fathomless dreaming, interrupted by the cries of something: Something warm from the living world of flesh and bone and blood.

The spirit of this ancient water elemental – an Undine – had roamed other planes and worlds for eons with its elemental brethren and only occasionally visited the middle world of the living things and when it did, it inhabited a strong-flowing stream, deep in the heart of a forest older than the memory or the stories of anything that crawled or walked or flew between or over it's venerable trees. But as it felt itself slide sideways into our world, it also felt that something had changed.

No longer did it feel the water tumbling, crashing and boiling. It could no longer feel the moving energy and simple power of the flowing water. The waterfall had stopped. It was stationary, static and gave a new sensation to being – it was solid. The waterfall had turned to ice.

The water elemental felt its spirit inhabit the frozen wall of ice and it refused to be held, so it took a step forward.

Anastasia heard a deep groaning sound – almost too deep for her ears to hear and it was more that she felt the sound through her body. From her spot in the back of the cave she could see the light change as it poured through the ice sheet in front of her: rainbow colours shifting and twisting, spots of light dilating and moving on the cave walls. Long cracks appeared in the ice and suddenly great sprays of frost exploded as, with the figure of giant man, the waterfall broke and took a step forward.

The ice giant, or Isoisä Jään as he was known later in the stories of the local people, turned, bending down and sending showers of frozen crystals into the air. He stared down at Anastasia, and Anastasia stared back up at him.

The ice giant was huge: great crags and geometric chunks overlaid each other to give the semblance of a vast, muscular human form, many times the height of a grown man. His eyes were deep, empty sockets and long icicles bearded his face. But she wasn't afraid.

She could feel his ancient power and somewhere inside herself she remembered the feeling of this great elemental spirit who had been present, comforting and warding, if invisible, when she had visited this place with her Grandfather.

The ice giant looked into the little girl's face, seeing the frozen tears on her cheeks sparkling in the winter sun, and looked into eyes that were as clear and pure and blue as the ice that made its own body. The child also stirred a memory: She reminded him of the white haired and long bearded human who could talk with him, in this forest place.

Now, the elemental didn't know much about humans, but it did know that this young one would not survive here, alone in this place. For the sake of the white bearded one, whose life presence it could no longer sense, the ice giant decided to help this child.

Scooping Anastasia up in its arms it strode, tall as a thatched house, through the winter forest, kicking up great fountains of snow with each stride, until it came upon another place of ancient gathering where a great ring of stones, carved by hands whose owners had been bones for thousands of years, encircled a hill top, bare of trees.

The winter sun was setting, and the thick snow clouds burned orange as the light began to fade and the ancient elemental set Anastasia down, against one of the tall stones.

Pointing to the southern edge of the circle and speaking in ways our bodies cannot hear, Isoisä Jään called upon its elemental cousin and a blisteringly hot being of pure fire, a Salamander, appeared, instantly melting the snow in a wide

circle around its licking, burning coils.

"I cannot care for this child", said Isoisä Jään in its own language. "Cousin Fire, can you take this child to your home and care for it?"

The Salamander of Fire laughed with a crackle, "I cannot take an animal to my home without destroying it and turning it to ash. Ask Cousin Air". And with that short exchange brought to an end, the elemental vanished, leaving only a wisp of steam from the thawed winter ground.

The ice giant turned to face the east, pointed and again spoke.

This time no fiery being appeared, but instead the surface snow was whipped into circles and only the merest suggestion of a flickering form hanging in the air, like a mirage, belied the presence of an elemental of air – a Sylph.

"I cannot care for this child", said Isoisä Jään again. "Cousin Air, can you take this child to your home and care for it?".

With words that to our ears would sound like a summer breeze through grass, the Sylph answered. "I cannot take an animal to my home that is not of the air. It is too cumbersome and would not survive. Ask Cousin Earth".

And the flying snow settled – the Sylph had left.

Again, the great water elemental turned and this time to the north. It pointed and spoke for the third time. In answer, the ground shuddered and a vast Gnome of earth rose up from the ground itself, with the sound like a distant earthquake, loose earth and stones rolling down the sides of the earth elemental that only just resembled a human figure.

"I cannot care for this child", said Isoisä Jään for the third time. "Cousin Earth, can you take this child to your home and care for it?".

The Gnome looked down at little Anastasia and paused before speaking, with a voice like rock grinding against rock.

"One day this child will come to the bosom of my home, under the earth, but that is not for many of her years yet. Until then she will travel on my back, but I will not bring her to my home now. Ask the animals, for those are her kind and they will be able to better care for her".

The earth elemental twisted back into the ground, the fallen soil and detritus flowing back into the hole and the turf curling back over, like gentle waves, to leave no mark of any disturbance in the ground.

Taking a moment, in the silence, to look over the top of the frozen forest, laid out and reaching in all directions to the horizon from the hill, the great frozen water elemental gently picked up Anastasia, cradling her in its indefatigable arms and strode back into the trees and walked the miles to a cave where a bear was sleeping.

"Bear!" called Isoisä Jään, waking the animal in its own language. "Bear! I cannot care for this child. Can you?"

The big brown bear roused from its winter slumber and blinked blearily at the little girl, who was very afraid of this huge and dangerous beast.

"She may sleep in my cave and I could keep her warm", yawned the bear. "But I have no food to give her and she would starve long before I woke in the spring. Ask the Wolves."

And with that, the creature rolled over, curled into a ball, tucked its snout under one of its gigantic arms and returned to its deep sleep.

Night had now come and the snow was falling thicker and thicker, spinning in long sweeps and clinging to the trees and smoothing the landscape to a flattened, rolling ocean of white.

When the ice giant reached the wolf pack and asked the same question as before, the huge, grizzled She Wolf replied that while she might have food enough, the child would probably freeze and certainly wouldn't be able to hold its own amongst the young and quickly growing wolf cubs. She suggested asking the Eagles.

Anastasia was now very hungry and very cold. Despite her thick furs she was shivering in the wind, her once rosy cheeks now the same colour as the snow drifts. These were things that Isoisä Jään had never had to consider before, but realised that finding something to care for the child in its charge was now urgent.

Standing with its head at the same level as the Eagles' nest, the ice giant spoke again, asking them for help. The birds were hunched down deep in their nest, keeping warm and avoiding the night wind and the freezing snow as best they could. They eyed Anastasia whose eyelids were now drooping as she clung to the body of ice.

"We cannot help you", said an Eagle. "This is a human child and should be with its own kind. Take it back to its own, where they can give it shelter and warmth and its own food".

The ice giant looked down into the face of the child. There were ice crystals on Anastasia's fur-trimmed hood and on her eyelashes. The pink colour she had had in her lips earlier now had more of a bluish cast and she appeared to be asleep.

The giant strode purposefully towards the nearest human habitation it could sense, but it had walked far in its journey to the stone circle and then to find the Bear, the Wolves and Eagles. After some hours more of walking, the whirling blizzard made navigation too confusing, even for this ancient being, and made its body of ice too brittle to maintain the strain that was being put upon it.

In the middle of the midnight forest, in the midst of a blizzard, Isoisä Jään, the frozen water elemental stopped walking.

It looked once more into the peaceful face of the child it had carried for miles and, bending its icy body and curving its icy limbs around, it crouched down on the forest floor, protecting its delicate charge as best it could and prepared to wait out the storm.

* * *

When morning came and the sun rose the storm had stopped.

As soon as it was light Anastasia's parents went straight back to the woods, taking neighbours and dogs with them, to search for their little daughter.

The neighbours exchanged meaningful looks and a shared understanding that it would need a miracle to find the little girl alive after a night in the blizzard-scoured forest, but they did their neighbourly duty anyway, if only for the sake of the girl's parents, and trudged into the deep snow, calling out and driving the dogs ahead of them.

* * *

Midday had passed and there was no sign of the girl, when the dogs suddenly became excited and started baying and barking, leaping through the deep snow, clearly on the trail of a scent.

With a burst of hope both the parents and their neighbours ran to follow the dogs who, after a few short but exhausting minutes of forging through the knee-deep snow, brought them to a place where mighty and ancient trees bent together to form a clearing, sheltered from the sky by the thick branches. In the middle of this clearing was mound where the snow had piled up against one side in a drift and it was round this the dogs were excitedly barking and scratching. The people now rushed up, looking at the strange shape.

They discovered the mound was a dome of ice, scoured smooth and low overnight by the driving snow. The dome wasn't one solid piece, but almost something like a seated or crouched figure, now worn down to a rough geometric shape. There were places where they could peer through tiny gaps between what looked something like branches or beams ... or limbs ... and inside, in the dim light filtering through the ice they could see the still form of a child – of Anastasia.

Some of the men brought their hatchets to bear on the ice, hacking away until they could reach inside. The interior of the dome was smooth, where the ice had melted and run down the inside and into the ground.

Anastasia's Mother and Father pulled her from this icy tomb, holding her close, crying out her name, their hot tears running onto her pale cheeks.

They held the still little form, the only sound in the quite, snow-bound forest was their grief.

Crying and crying they held her until, like the miracle they had prayed for, they saw her eyes flicker open – she was alive!

Cold, hungry and lonely, Anastasia had survived the night in the winter forest.

The being that had protected her and sheltered her had now gone back to its own world.

Not just for the sake of a now dead shaman, but having looked into eyes of glacial blue and seen frozen tears of crystalised water, Anastasia – this little girl – had melted the ice giant's heart.

The Lost Lady of The Pines

There is a land, where the summers are short, the winters are long and full of ice, and the forest covers all; and in many parts of that country, like any other visitor, the dead are always welcome at the hearth.

Not the bones or bodies that are simply the mortal carriage, but the shades of those dear-departed who have not yet crossed over, who may still have purpose, and are sorely missed by those they left behind.

As the fruitful year dies away and the first snows are soon to fall, there are many homes where, on one particular late autumn night, a glass of strong spirits and a honeyed cake are left at the hearth for the dead, who are welcomed to that home or hall.

Now, there are some who say this is just a tradition and a way of finding solace in memory, but there are others who say that in the morning the hearth has been swept, a new fire laid and the drink and the cake are gone.

Not so peaceful is the hereafter for those whose graves are unmarked; whose bodies were not laid to rest with kindness and tears: Those who were lost in the forest and lost forever.

Lost, like the young woman, whose house was burned on her wedding night; her new husband slain as he lay in her arms, leaving her to run from their attackers; run into the night, and run deep into the forest.

No quiet, tended grave or honeyed cakes for the young wife's ghost, but the unending pain of her lost love, her wedding gown torn and taken to line the nests of crows, her bones gnawed by foxes, pierced by tree roots, clothed in velvet moss and studded with garnet mushrooms that soften and blacken in the winter, among the quiet of the forest pines.

* * *

Some years later another young woman was on her way to be married. She was travelling from her village to that of her betrothed, and escorted by her two brothers and their Father.

Although they stayed on the path, it was deep in the forest and far from help that they were set upon. The men fought bravely, allowing their sister, their daughter, time to escape as she fled into the trees.

But the attackers followed her, baying like hounds, knowing it was only time before the girl weakened and they would fall upon her.

The pillared trunks of the pines grew closer and closer and the light from the sun grew fainter and fainter, as hunter and hunted pushed deeper and deeper into the forest's heart. Tiring, the young woman fell, stumbling, gasping for breath, onto the soft, deep, pungent carpet of needles.

As she fell, she didn't notice that her hand closed around a finger bone, lying, thinly covered, on the forest floor; a finger bone that still bore a ring, a wedding ring.

The young woman got to her feet again, unthinkingly clutching the finger bone and its ring, but this time when she ran, gossamer strands of mist followed in her wake, fanning out behind her, like the train of a dress.

Her pursuers didn't notice the mist. They didn't notice it growing and thickening around their ankles. In the heat of the chase they didn't feel the unseasonal cold, dragging its nails down their legs.

Finally the young woman was cornered.

In a forest hollow, against a low and ragged cliff, exhaustion took her and she fell down into the white vapours and they closed over and covered her.

The hunters slowed, knowing the chase was won, grinning and hungry for their prize.

But the figure that stood up out of the pool of mist was not their quarry.

Glowing white shreds of chill fog rolled off the shoulders of the female form, hugging her like a silk gown. But it was the sight of her body that made the men stand as still as the trees that surrounded them: Roots and sticks and leaves and moss and stones and the creatures that crawl and wriggle through the litter of the forest floor combined to make a sketch of bones and hair and knotted, gnarly sinew. If, in life, she had ever been beautiful, she was now terrible to look upon and a host to long-brooded vengeance.

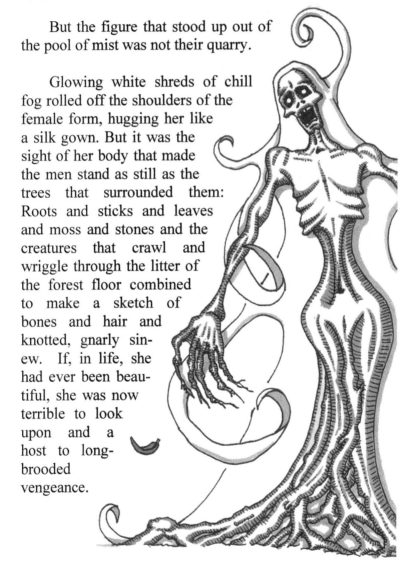

In the pregnant, fear-filled silence a quiet creak was heard, like a branch in a night breeze, as vines and roots moved and twisted to allow the hideous figure to open wide, her mouldered mouth.

And then she screamed.

And as she screamed all the horrors of the night poured from that terrible maw and the air was filled with the shrieking of bats and clouds of flapping moths and the howls of wolves and skittering, blood-eyed rats poured forth and ran like black sanguine down her front.

Those men who did not – or could not – run, themselves screaming, into the forest to meet their own, lonely fates were held fast where they stood; not just immobilised by fear, but bound to the ground by reaching roots that sprang up through the floor, wrapping around their legs and bodies.

Great boughs of trees swept down and beat and broke them. Small animals crept from holes and burrows and ravaged their flesh, and all the while the entangling roots squeezed the breath from their bodies and popped their bones.

And as all this was happening, the men who now wept and called for their Mothers could do nought but watch the ghastly spectre as she slowly processed towards them until, as their pain and fear was at its worst and their own warm blood slid wet and hot down their broken bodies, she came to kiss each of

them in turn; a kiss that was filled with the sweetness

of leaf mould, as pine needles and soft earth poured into their mouths and filled their throats.

* * *

When the young woman awoke it was to find herself not far from the path she had fled from. Her Father, with a bloodied, makeshift bandage around his head woke her and held her, before he took her back to where her wounded brothers were resting.

She couldn't remember how she had escaped or how she had found her way back. She couldn't even remember where she had found the ring that she was now wearing next to her little finger, on her left hand.

But later, after she was happily married, her own wedding ring worn alongside the ring from the forest, what she did know was that her babies slept sounder and longer than any of her neighbours'. And that on an autumn night, if a honeyed cake and a glass of strong spirits were left out for the dead, the next morning her hearth was as clean as it had ever been and the fire that was now laid there burned longer and hotter than any she could ever lay.

And no man or beast or wolf ever came out of the forest to bother that village again, for a whole generation.

The Toad's Tale

There is a country far to the north and far to the east of here, where the mammoth roam, and it is sometimes too cold to snow. These great beasts graze on the frozen tundra grasses, dreaming of the summertime and fresh green shoots.

Further south from the ice plains, where the forest grows thick and dark, generations ago people cleared the ground in places and, when the sun warms the soil, crops can be farmed to feed the people of that country, to make their bread, to brew their beer and their spirits, and to feed their animals.

It was in one such place that a feast was being held. And in this place and at this feast there was a Wise One who, it was rumoured, could speak with the trees, the clouds and the animals of the field.

When everyone had eaten their fill, the candles had burned low and even the musicians were nodding in their seats, two rich farmers were enjoying an argument about which of them had the best animals on their farm.

"Why, my cattle are the largest and most tender in the Empire", said one.

"Well, my pigs are the fattest and the most toothsome in the World!" cried the other.

And this went backward and forward for some time until they had both run out of words to describe their increasingly wondrous and ever more fantastically worthy stock.

Finally one of the farmers turned to the Wise One with the gift of knowing all that is living, who was currently staring into the depths of his cup, and asked, "Wise One: My cousin says he has the best animals on his farm, whereas I know I have the best animals on my farm. How can we settle this matter?"

The room quietened as all eyes, now waking from their hearthside dozing turned, their owners curious to hear what the Wise One had to say.

For a few moments the man was silent, and some wondered if he'd heard the question. But then he simply answered, "Easy. You both have the best animal on your farms, but neither of you has mentioned Him tonight".

"My Bull!" said the first farmer. But the Wise One shook his head.

"My Boar?" hoped the second. But again the Wise One shook his head.

The farmers exchanged confused glances and asked the man to tell them what it was they both had, that was the best of all animals.

By way of an answer, the Wise One dipped his hand into the cup he'd been staring into, scooped up its contents, and then opened his hand.

A young girl near him made an involuntary squeal and an Old Father close by wrinkled his nose in disgust and disapproval, as sitting, calmly, in the centre of the Wise One's palm was a toad.

"But that is just old Sagbelly; he is of no value to me", said the first farmer.

"How can old Wartskin be a great animal, when he is so small and ugly?" asked the second.

"I was once told a story", said the Wise One looking at the toad and smiling, "Of two animals who asked and said such things as you, and how they were proved wrong".

The toad sat quietly on his hand, watching all that was happening with his great, golden eyes, the only movement his throat, beating with his breath.

And this is the story the Wise One told…

* * *

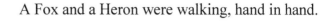

A Fox and a Heron were walking, hand in hand.

They were very much in love and regularly told each other so.

But in reality they were more in love with themselves than each other: The Fox was so proud of his thick red fur and bushy tail, but secretly harboured thoughts of sinking his fine white teeth into the Heron's plump breast. The Heron preened and fussed with her sleek plumage and liked to watch the reflections of her long legs when she went wading in the water, but often wished to pluck those glowing amber orbs from the Fox's head, with her long, sharp beak, and swallow them whole.

On this day, the Fox and the Heron had come to the edge of the forest and were looking across a field of sun-yellow corn, ripening in the already fading summer.

At the edge of this field, at the edge of the forest, was a great beech tree and between its shady roots, each as thick as a man's leg, lived a Toad.

Coming to rest against the tree, the Fox yelped as he found he'd stood upon the Toad, unseen by him, so well was his jacket matched to the colours and shapes of the forest floor.

"How disgusting!" croaked the Heron.

"What an awful thing", moaned the Fox.

But the Toad said nothing and merely watched.

"You are the perfect mirror of ugliness to my lovely Heron", said the Fox, and the Heron simpered modestly.

"Why", she said, "Perhaps I should snap you up in my long beak, for besmirching my handsome Fox's sleek and soft paw!"

And the Fox smiled coyly and tipped his head in recognition of the compliment.

"Tell me", said the Fox, "Why I should not set my fine, white teeth to you for the insult of your existence? Explain yourself!" he demanded.

"Explain myself?" asked the Toad, his sparkling eyes turning, seemingly, to look at both animals at once.

"Quite so!" Squeaked the Heron and busied herself with grooming her wing.

The Toad sighed and began to recite, as if this had happened many times before:

> *My soul is old,*
> *My eyes are gold,*
> *And see all the World around me.*
> *My pockets are filled,*
> *With potions and pills,*
> *I am a castle to confound thee.*

The Fox and the Heron didn't know what to think and laughed nervously to cover their confusion.

The Toad watched and waited.

"I do believe this odious little creature is mocking us, my Dear", said the Fox, trying to recover his natural feeling of superiority.

"I do believe he thinks himself better than us!" said the Heron, fanning her dismay with one wing.

"Not better. Not worse. Just different", said the Toad ... as a matter of fact.

Both the Fox and the Heron gasped, trying to disguise their bafflement.

"I should take you to my brother's cubs and let them play with you! He has six cubs ... *six*, mark you!" shouted the Fox, becoming increasingly excited.

"You could. But should I let my children find and play with you in your den? And my children number in their hundreds", replied the Toad.

"I should fling you into the field and let the sun crack your slimy skin!" screeched the horrified Heron.

"You could. But I would dig myself into the soft earth and sleep until the moon is risen. The earth is my home and where I sleep past the fangs of the sun and even the claws of winter", replied the Toad … as a matter of fact … and stayed where he was, in the shade of the tree, watching the boastful, petulant animals and gazing over the swaying corn.

"I am hated", the Toad continued, "Because some find me ugly. But those whose sight goes beyond shape, and sees an individual's true worth know me better.

"The farmer whose land this is loves me and my family and our ways. For him we fight a war for which no medals are won and no titles given. I fight a war against the things that crawl and slither, that spring and chitter. Things that would take the crops from the farmer, the crops that give cover to you, Fox, and are the home for unlucky prey for you, Heron.

"While some seek to outdo others, and be seen as virtuous above them, I watch and I wait. And when the time is right …".

At this point, and with perfect serendipity, a cricket hopped by. Without disturbing his composure, the Toad flashed out his tongue – twice the length of his body – and swallowed the pest in a single gulp, blinking as he did.

"… I act", he finished.

"How beastly!" wailed the Heron.

"How presumptuous!" snarled the Fox and snapped the Toad up in his gleaming white teeth. But before he had a chance to swallow him the Fox began to splutter and spit and flung the hapless animal from his jaws, onto the forest floor.

"What poison is this?" cried the Fox, retching and gagging.

"I told you, '*My pockets are filled, with potions and pills*'", repeated the toad, rubbing the remnants of the sticky poisons off the warts on his back and cleaning his hands on some dry leaves.

"My Dear! My only! What did he do to you?" crooned the Heron, while the Fox tried to remove the foul taste from his mouth by crunching on some green leaves.

The Heron watched the Toad with narrowing eyes as he sat perfectly still.

"I have no need to bight or chew", she said slyly, and then, quick as summer lightening, her head darted forward on her slender neck and she had the Toad in her beak. High in the air she tossed him, opening her scissored mouth, ready to swallow him whole, but something miraculous had happened. The small creature had swelled and grown to more than twice his original size and instead of disappearing down the Heron's throat he caught in her beak, causing her eyes to bulge, goggling at her own, open-mouthed misfortune.

The Heron shook her head, dislodging the toad who, falling to the forest floor once more, let out his breath and starting to shrink to his normal size repeated the words, *"'I am a castle to confound thee'"*.

Shocked, shamed and still spitting out foul-tasting liquid, the Fox and the Heron left without another word, consoling each other in their distress and casting dark and meaningful glances behind them. The Toad, who'd decided he'd had enough adventure for one day, retired to his home beneath the tree roots, closing the door on the whimpering, simpering dandies and enjoyed the cool and the dark.

* * *

Some days, not long after this meeting, the farmer, whose field it was at the edge of the forest, was very pleased to give his wife a handsome new fox fur he'd made, especially after the meal she'd provided for him and their children, of succulent roast heron.

Meanwhile, the Toad pulled his jacket straight around his broad body and, while some of the other animals squawked and preened, and pranced and postured, he remained vigilant, watching the world through his shining golden eyes and using his great and timeless wisdom to know when to listen, when to watch, when to wait … and when to act.

The Kelpie's Bridle

We are by the side of a large pool, nestled between steep-sided granite mountains: grey, rugged and sparsely covered with heather and rough grass. The water is dark with peat, ice-cold and said to be bottomless. The shoreline is made of scattered grey rocks, pebbles and boulders that have tumbled from the mountainsides. A young woman kneels on the shore right next to the water's edge; her name is Caitrìona. She is beautiful, with copper-red hair, milk-white skin and eyes of green fairy fire; but these eyes are rimmed with red as she is crying – sobbing. Less than an hour ago she watched the man she loved drown.

* * *

Tadhg had asked Caitrìona if she'd like to go for a walk. He'd been unusually nervous and wouldn't say why he'd particularly wanted to go for a walk on that day, but the two of them had been inseparable since infancy and she'd happily agreed.

To anyone else, it was clear that they loved each other and were destined for a future life together. This was clear to all, especially to Bhreac who also loved Caitrìona and would happily see Tadgh out of the way, not that either of the young lovers knew this.

That morning Tadgh had arrived at Caitrìona's house dressed in the full eight yards of cloth that made up his family's tartan, pinned at the shoulder of a smart, new linen shirt with a brooch that was an heirloom that had belonged to his Father, and his Father's Fathers for many generations before. He was a young man, tall enough to be handsome without being intimidating, good looking enough to be attractive without overshadowing Caitrìona's looks and his family owned a good-sized plot of crofting land.

He took his young lover by the hand and they walked over the hills and tussocky grazing land towards the lonely pool. They both knew of its existence, but old stories about its unplumbable depths and the fay that haunted that area kept most people away.

Tadgh prattled aimlessly as they walked, occasionally his hand would stray to his sleeve where, unseen by Caitrìona, he would fuss with a small and delicate item hidden there. As they reached the basin in the mountains where the pool lay, the great cliffs frowning over it's smooth, obsidian surface, Tadgh gave a shout and pointed.

Champing the grass not far from the water was a beautiful white horse. Bearing no tack, harness or brand, the horse, as the young man said, must be wild and not *currently* owned by anyone.

"I will capture it and make it a present for you. A special present", he finished with a wink and a shy smile.

Caitrìona was both confused and flattered, and protested that he shouldn't be so stupid or do such a dangerous thing, but the young man, being a young man with his young lady watching, didn't heed any words of warning and was resolved to prove his worth.

He stepped slowly up to the horse; its hide was white as starlight, its mane flowed and drifted in the air like gossamer, its flanks rippled with powerful muscles. Holding out his hand, he approached the animal from the front. It nuzzled his upturned palm with its velvet nose and he moved closer to stroke its neck and whisper quiet words of comfort and reassurance.

Caitrìona held her breath. Tadgh seemed to be charming the horse as it stood placidly, allowing him to move down its flanks and lean against its side. He turned, grinning at Caitrìona before easing himself onto the animal's back and sitting proudly like a Celtic Chieftain of old.

"Caitrìona!" the young man called out. "I claim this beast in your name and offer it to you as a gift - my gift for ...". His next words 'for our wedding day, if you'll have me', were cut off as, suddenly, the horse reared and bolted.

Now, when a horse bolts you hold on. To try and get off can mean great injury, especially hitting granite-strewn ground from the back of a fast moving mount, and Tadgh knew this.

He gripped the animal's sides with his knees, clutched handfuls of its mane and bent low to its back, trying to steer it in a circle to bring it under control.

But this was no ordinary horse. With a fierce and supernatural strength and will it sped straight towards the pool, leaping into the shallows and plunging into the depths, down, down into the brown water. Tadgh was dragged down, down with the beast until there was nothing left but bubbles on the surface.

The young man had been dragged into the depths and to his doom by a water horse – by a kelpie.

* * *

After Caitríona had sat and wept until she could weep no more she stood, looked at the glassy-smooth surface of the pool one last time, and turned and walked away.

She had no plan as to where she was walking, but simply walked, heading further into the mountains, numb with shock. She walked and walked, her arms hanging limply by her sides and her eyes blank and pitiful, until she came to a mountain stream.

Instead of being a tumbling, roiling ribbon of crystal-clear water, this stream ran red with blood, and the site of this brought the young woman out of her despondent reverie with a jolt.

Looking upstream, she could see a figure, crouching at the stream's edge, industriously working away and the blood was flowing from where this figure was.

Cautiously approaching, it became clear that the figure was dressed in green and was washing bloodstained clothes in the cold mountain water. This must be the Caointeach – a fay, known by many names and a portent of death, and found in lonely places such as this, washing the bloody clothes of those who were about to die.

Caitríona felt sure the clothes the Caointeach was washing belonged to Tadgh, whose beautiful manly body was even now being torn apart and consumed by the kelpie after it had drowned him in the depths of the mountain pool, and she walked, in a trance, to where the bent figure was hard at work.

She reached the Caointeach without her notice and, peering over the hag's shoulder, she could see the gore-sodden clothing – a night-blue coat with bright, brass buttons – as she plunged it into the water of the stream again and again, before slapping it onto a flat rock and scrubbing, leaving scarlet trails that drifted and twisted and span together in the once clear stream.

"These are not the clothes of my precious man", said the young woman flatly as she looked at the unfamiliar garment.

The Caointeach started, turning to face Caitrìona. She was hideous, with great aged, sagging flaps of skin hanging in folds, like curtains of flesh from her sunken jowls and scrawny throat. Her eyes were pinpoints of silver-grey mica, glittering angrily from yellowed, oyster-rimmed sockets and her hair hung in thin, greasy-grey rat-tails on her shoulders. Her gnarled and lumpen hands protectively clutched the green gown she wore about her, but not close enough to cover her great, webbed feet.

"Of course they're not, foolish child!" screeched the Caointeach, revealing her single remaining tooth, crooked and brown like bogwood in her puckered hole of a mouth.

"These are the clothes of a man yet to die, whereas your foolish goat of a boy is neither dead, nor is he soon to be!".

Caitrìona rocked, shaken to her core. She had seen Tadgh carried into the pool, under its waters, and he had not appeared again. "Not dead!", she cried. "Then he is alive?"

"Yes, yes, he's very much alive an' sitting on his own in an air-filled cave beneath the mountain pool", replied the Caointeach in her pinched and cracked voice. "But before y' ask me anythin' else, know that I will answer ye three things and no more – and you've just had one so you've got only two left. Choose carefully before y' go matherin' and blatherin' and cluckin' out foolish things, for I'll no' here your complaints after".

The young woman stopped, thought for a moment then asked, "If my Tadgh is not dead, how do I rescue him?"

"That'll do, hen", chuckled the Caointeach, pleased the young woman had chosen her question well. "D' y' know the great boulder that is known as The Long Man's Anvil?"

Caitrìona nodded.

"D' y' know why it's known as the Long Man's Anvil?"

Caitrìona shook her head.

"Because, beneath that great stone is a vast cave. And in that cave is a blacksmith. But this is no ordinary blacksmith – not that any blacksmith is ordinary – but this smith is a giant. They say the stone was put there by the Devil, or Saint Michael – or one of his lot – as a punishment, and he's trapped there, and when he rings his great hammer on the anvil in his cave, it sounds like thunder in the mountaintops.

"You must go to the giant and ask him to make you a bridle of metal links – of cold iron – to trap the fairy horse. Then, cover the bridle in blood to hide the smell of cold iron and to tempt the kelpie that took your man to come to you. Go to meet it near its pool and climb upon its back.

"As it did with your damn fool of a boy, it will rush into the deep water and drag you down. Let it. When you are under the water pull the bridle onto its head – if you do it above the water, it'll throw you or change form and escape. Once the bridle is on, command it to take you to your man before your breath runs out and don't let go of beast nor bridle until you're both back on dry land!".

"Thank you!" cried Caitrìona, her heart bursting with hope and she turned to run to find the great stone.

"Do you no' want your last question?" asked the Caointeach with a twinkle in her spritely eyes.

Caitrìona paused and then, "Yes. Why didn't the kelpie kill and eat my Tadgh?"

The Caointeach gave a gummy grin - she'd been hoping Caitrìona would ask this.

"Today Tadgh was going to ask you to marry him, and he confided this to one he thought a friend. But that wee man has also set his cap at you, and tricked Tadgh into believing a great gift was needed to win your hand – the gift of a white horse and he knew just where he could find a wild one to capture and call your own.

"Now, so's not to be haunted by a vengeful ghost this man made a deal with the kelpie not to kill, but to take young Tadgh and hide him in an underwater cave, promising him fresh meat in the future with Tadgh as security. This other man's name is Bhreac".

"Aye", continued the Caointeach at Caitrìona's gasp. "The same Bhreac as has been a friend to you both since you were young".

The Caointeach's cackling bounced from wall to wall of the unforgiving mountains as Caitrìona turned, sobbing, and fled, in the direction of the great stone known as The Long Man's Anvil.

* * *

At the foot of a mist-topped and snow-capped mountain lay an enormous boulder. Big as a Laird's hall it sat, silent and immovable, resting in a hollow of some sort. How was Caitrìona to find any way to lift it to get underneath? There must be a hidden way in.

Five minutes of searching brought only the discovery of a ragged and rangy hawthorn tree. The poor thing seemed to be squeezing out from under the rock, its reaching roots like grasping fingers, curling over the unyielding granite surface. But, on closer inspection, and peering between the crawling limbs, she realized she could see down, deep into the earth – the roots spanned a tunnel leading directly down and under the great boulder.

Scraping her body as she wriggled down into the tangle of roots, Caitrìona found the network of rope-like tendrils quickly opened up allowing her to climb deeper and deeper, like clambering over rough and fibrous rigging.

Twenty feet, forty feet, sixty feet and more she climbed down until the network thinned out to only a few roots, hanging together and twisting around each other and making a very convenient ladder of sorts.

This ladder brought her down through a hole in the ceiling and onto the floor of a huge cave. In the middle was an anvil as large as a cow. A red, infernal glow lit the space, from a titanic, forge on the other side of the space, casting long and gently flickering deep shadows that obscured the identity of the objects and equipment arrayed around the room's edge.

The air was stiflingly hot and rank with the reek of old sweat.

She picked her way carefully towards the great anvil and in answer to her timid 'hello?', a bulky

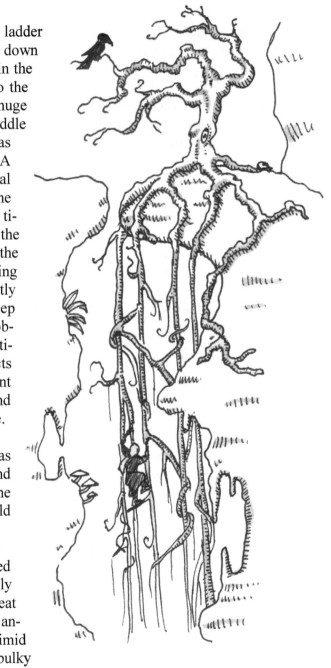

mass moved in the shadows. First it was round and impossible to determine what it belonged to, but it rapidly unfurled. With the red-hot coals behind it, making its outline shimmer in the heat, the shape resolved into that of a man, but a man many, *many* times larger than any Caitrìona had met.

She thought the giant would never stop, but eventually he stood at his full height, twice that of a barn door; sweat glistened on his brawny arms, his hair and beard were long and shaggy like un-carded fleece; his eyes, reflecting the forge light, seemed to glow

with a demonic intensity; but the thing that caught her attention was a thick collar of bright silver around its throat.

"Why has a little mortal girl foolishly strayed into my smithy?" boomed the giant in a deep and sonorous voice, sounding like boulders being dropped into the ocean.

He loomed over her; this close she could see his pale skin grimed with dirt and soot, the smell of his unclean body in this sweltering room was almost overpowering, and she realised that if she wanted to escape, she would never be able to climb the ladder of roots to safety before the giant simply plucked her off and bit her in half.

Caitrìona was terrified, but she'd come here to do a job and, best as she could, she summoned up her courage, firmly planted her feet, stuck out her chin and made her demand.

"I need you to make me a bridle of cold iron to catch a kelpie!"

The giant chuckled, not unkindly, in reply but also rubbed his finger along the inside of the heavy silver collar he wore – it looked sore.

"Why do you wear that collar?" she asked.

"Not out of choice", replied the giant. "No: Centuries ago, before you tiny people came to my Isles, I smithed a sword for a demon, to use in war against the angels. To punish me, an angelic smith made this collar of silver, which has held about my throat ever since. I cannot file nor strike it off, but every time I do a good deed in the eyes of the angels, the collar gets loser. One day I will have done my penance and be able to slip it over my head. Until then, for my sins, it does not allow me to leave my forge, or it chokes me".

"Well, you can do a good deed and help me to rescue my man?" said Caitrìona feeling bolder now.

"You must always give something in exchange for my work, and what will you give me?" asked the giant, folding his broad arms across his chest.

Her mind went blank. Caitrìona hadn't thought this far.

"I … I have no money with me, no jewelry, no valuables of any kind. I have nothing to give," she started.

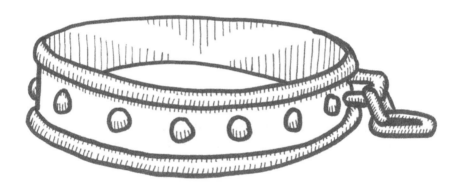

The giant reached out his hand, as big as a hogshead barrel and with as much gentleness as he could manage ran Caitrìona's hair over his fingers, before straightening up and taking a breath, a look of consideration on his face.

"If you will willingly give me twelve hairs from your fiery head I will make you your bridle of cold iron", he said.

"Of course", replied Caitrìona, wondering. "But what for?
"I will beat them and meld them with gold and draw them into wire and wind them into harp strings for the angels and maybe they will forgive me a little more".

So Caitríona plucked twelve of the longest hairs from her head and gave them to the giant. Then, she sat in a corner away from the forge as the huge smith pumped bellows the size of ox carts, making the coals blaze furiously before smelting and hammering until he had made a bridle of iron, plunging it into a barrel of water with hiss, to cool and temper it.

When he handed it to Caitríona, she asked that he lay his knife on the top of the anvil. To her, it was as long as a sword and with the point pricked her palms, running the cold iron bridle through her hands to smother it in her blood, before climbing up and out of the cave, back to the world above.

* * *

The young woman approached the dark pool quietly, cautiously looking from side to side until she saw the kelpie, innocent and beautiful-looking in its horse form, grazing peacefully near the water's edge. She backtracked and circled round, until she was approaching the animal from upwind, hoping the scent of her blood would both disguise the cold iron bridle hidden in her clothing, and tempt the monster.

It worked.

The beast's nostrils flared, catching the ferrous smell, and it lifted its head and looked in her direction. She smiled sweetly, and walked slowly towards it. In return the kelpie calmly walked in her direction and allowed Caitríona to stroke its head, subtly licking at her palms as it did.

Walking slowly down its side, she reached a point where she could jump and then hoist herself onto its back.

As before, with Tadgh, as soon as she was astride the kelpie it bolted and headed for the water, kicking up wild fountains of spray with its hooves and then, with Caitrìona clinging desperately to its back, it plunged into the depths.

Fighting the urge to gasp as she hit the freezing water, she was dragged down, down, down, silvery bubbles tickling past her face and the increasing water pressure squeezing the air in her lungs and making her ears ache.

Now, desperately and both as quickly and as carefully as she could she pulled the cold iron bridle that the giant had forged for her from inside her clothing.

The kelpie sensed it instantly and she felt it panic, but before it could change form or rise to the surface or do anything else, she deftly slipped it over its muzzle and pulled it tight against its cheeks, the bit sliding into its mouth as it fought against the burning, binding iron.

"Take me to my man, before my breath runs out!" screamed Caitrìona and though to her ears all she could hear was a bubbling, gargling cacophony the beast seem to understand.

At the point where lights began to burst in front of her eyes and she felt sure her body would betray her and make her gasp in lungfuls of brown water the kelpie breached the surface, inside a small cave and she had never been so pleased to feel cold air rush into her breath-starved body.

The cave was lit with a low glow from phosphorescent mushrooms that studded the walls and in the dim light she saw Tadgh, standing up in alarm, staring in amazement and admiration as

Caitriona, still astride the bone-white fairy horse, shook the water from her beautiful hair and smiled at him.

* * *

Short minutes later Tadgh was wringing the water from his kilt on, the shore, watching as Caitriona stripped the cold iron bridle from the kelpie's head. It revealed a nasty, red burn scar where it had crisscrossed the beast's face and no sooner was it free of the bridle than it dove into the depths until, again, there were only bubbles left on surface.

Caitriona and Tadgh held each other and wept. Wept with relief at end of their adventure; wept as they rejoiced at Tadgh's return to safety, and for their reunion.

"I think you hadn't finished what you were saying, when you got stolen away", said Caitriona smiling up into Tadgh's eyes.

Feeling a fear almost as great as that of being kidnapped by a man-eating water monster, Tadgh chewed his lip, feeling in his sleeve for the object he had concealed there.

"Caitriona: I have always loved you and if you'll have me, I would like you to be my wife", he said, holding out a beautiful filigree necklace of silver and moonstones that had been his original wedding gift to her.

"I will", she cried, holding up her hair so he could put the necklace on her. "I will. And I would fight a thousand kelpies to be your wife".

And so, together they went back to their village, cold, wet, tired, but very much in love.

* * *

Yes, Tadgh confronted Bhreac about his deception, but where was the proof? Stories of kelpies and mountain hags and imprisoned giants were met with scorn and disbelieving smiles. In the end fists were flung and noses were bloodied, but little else was done and everyone moved on with their lives.

One day, not too long after this, Tadgh and Caitríona were married. They exchanged their vows in front of their families and their friends and the rest of the village and a feast was held in their honour.

And as the night fell, and the guests settled into their cups, and danced and laughed and drank, no one noticed the arrival of a stranger, dressed in clothes as white as starlight, with hair as white and fine as gossamer, eyes as black as a bottomless mountain pool, baring strange crisscross scars on his face and what looked like water weeds trailing behind him. Nor did anyone notice him approach Bhreac who was dressed in a smart, new night-blue coat with bright, brass buttons. Certainly no one saw what happened next as Bhreac's debt was settled; nor, for that matter, did anyone ever see Bhreac again.

But for Caitríona and Tadgh they both lived full and loving married lives and had many children and grandchildren.

And they both lived happily ever after.

Lightning Source UK Ltd.
Milton Keynes UK
UKHW02f0044200218
318144UK00004B/161/P